全民阅读·经典小丛书

飞鸟集

[印] 泰戈尔 著　冯慧娟 编

Stray Birds

吉林出版集团股份有限公司

图书在版编目（CIP）数据

飞鸟集 / (印) 泰戈尔著; 冯慧娟编. — 长春 : 吉林出版集团股份有限公司，2015.6（2025.1重印）
（全民阅读. 经典小丛书）
ISBN 978-7-5534-7585-1

Ⅰ. ①飞… Ⅱ. ①泰… ②冯… Ⅲ. ①诗集 – 印度 – 现代 Ⅳ. ①I351.25

中国版本图书馆 CIP 数据核字 (2015) 第 119870 号

FEI NIAO JI

飞鸟集

作　　者：［印］泰戈尔　著　冯慧娟　编
出版策划：崔文辉
选题策划：冯子龙
责任编辑：金佳音
排　　版：新华智品
出　　版：吉林出版集团股份有限公司
（长春市福祉大路 5788 号，邮政编码：130118）
发　　行：吉林出版集团译文图书经营有限公司
（http://shop34896900.taobao.com）
电　　话：总编办 0431-81629909　营销部 0431-81629880 / 81629881
印　　刷：吉林省金昇印务有限公司
开　　本：640mm × 940mm 1/16
印　　张：10
字　　数：130 千字
版　　次：2015 年 7 月第 1 版
印　　次：2025 年 1 月第 4 次印刷
书　　号：ISBN 978-7-5534-7585-1
定　　价：48.00 元

印装错误请与承印厂联系　电话：18604312011

前言

《飞鸟集》是泰戈尔的代表作，也是世界上最杰出的诗集之一。译者郑振铎曾深情地盛赞这部诗集“包涵着深邃的大道理”，“像山坡草地上的一丛丛的野花，在早晨的太阳光下，纷纷地伸出头来。随你喜爱什么吧，那颜色和香味是多种多样的。”

泰戈尔（Rabindranath Tagore，1861年——1941年），印度诗人、小说家、戏剧家、社会活动家。1913年，他自译的英文版《吉檀迦利》出版，轰动世界，并在次年荣获诺贝尔文学奖，是亚洲获得此项奖的第一人。从此，他的作品被译成多国文字，广为流传。泰戈尔一生中共写了50多部诗集，12部中、长篇小说，100多篇短篇小说，20多个剧本，此外，他还创作了大量文史类论著，其作品博大精深，奠定了印度近代文学的基础，也为东方文学赢得了世界声誉。

Preface

《飞鸟集》是一部英文格言诗集，共收录诗歌325首，完成于1916年。这部诗集的内容包罗万象，语言简洁凝练，清新质朴，意味隽永，诗人将白昼和黑夜、溪流和海洋、自由和背叛巧妙地合二为一，引领世人探寻真理和智慧的源泉。正如美籍华人学者周策纵先生所说，“它们真像海滩上晶莹的鹅卵石，每一颗自有一个天地。它们是零碎的、短小的；但却是丰富的、深刻的。”

为了方便读者阅读，我们将《飞鸟集》以中英文对照的形式辑录在一起，其中的英文部分系诗人原译，中文为中国文学家郑振铎亲译。相信在两位大师的引导下，您在欣赏经典诗歌的同时，一定能在潜移默化中提高自己的英文水平。

Preface

飞鸟集

Fei Niao Ji

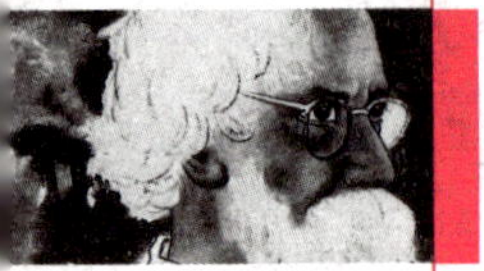

1

Stray birds of summer come to my window to sing and fly away.

And yellow leaves of autumn， which have no songs， flutter and fall there with a sign.

夏天的飞鸟，飞到我的窗前唱歌，又飞去了。

秋天的黄叶，它们没有什么可唱，只叹息一声，飞落在那里。

2

On troupe of little vagrants of the world， leave your footprints in my words.

世界上的一队小小的漂泊者呀，请在我的文字里留下你们的足印。

3

The world puts off its mask of vastness to its lover.

It becomes small as one song， as one kiss of the eternal.

世界对着它的爱人，把它浩瀚的面具揭下了。

它变小了，小如一首歌，小如一个永恒的吻。

4

It is the tears of the earth that keep her smiles in bloom.

是大地的泪点，使她的微笑保持着青春不谢。

5

The mighty desert is burning for the love of a blade of grass who shakes her head and laughs and flies away.

无垠的沙漠热烈地追求一叶绿草的爱，可是她摇摇头，笑着飞走了。

6

If you shed tears when you miss the sun, you also miss the stars.

如果你因错过太阳而流泪，那么你也要错过群星了。

7

The sands in your way beg for your song and your movement, dancing water.

Will you carry the burden of their lameness?

舞动中的流水呀，途中的泥沙在请求你的歌声、你的流动呢。

你肯挟跛足的泥沙一同远行吗?

8

Her wishful face haunts my dreams like the rain at night.

她的热切的脸，如夜雨似的，搅扰着我的梦魂。

9

Once we dreamt that we were strangers.

We wake up to find that we were dear to each other.

有一次，我们梦见大家都是不相识的。

我们醒了，却知道我们原是相亲相爱的。

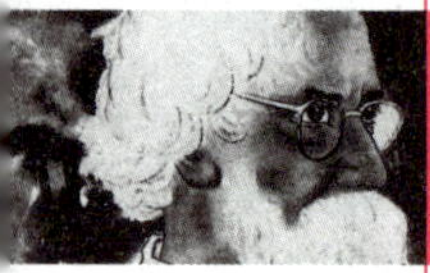

10

Sorrow is hushed into peace in my heart like the evening among the silent trees.

忧思在我的心里平静下去，正如暮色降临在寂静的山林中。

11

Some unseen fingers, like an idle breeze, are playing upon my heart the music of the ripples.

有些看不见的手指，如懒懒的微飔似的，正在我的心头上，奏着潺湲的乐声。

12

“What language is thine, O sea? ”

“The language of eternal question. ”

“What language is thy answer, O sky? ”

“The language of eternal sile–nce. ”

“海水呀，你说的是什么？”

“是永恒的疑问。”

“天空呀，你的回答是什么？”

“是永恒的沉默。”

13

Listen, my heart, to the whispers of the world with which it makes love to you.

静静地听，我的心呀，听那世界的低语，这是它对你的爱的表示呀。

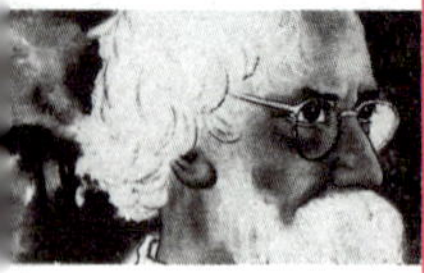

14

The mystery of creation is like the darkness of night——it is great.

Delusions of knowledge are like the fog of the morning.

创造的神秘，有如夜间的黑暗——是伟大的。

而知识的幻影，不过是晨间之雾。

15

Do not seat your love upon a precipice because it is high.

不要因为峭壁是高的，便让你的爱情坐在峭壁上。

16

I sit at my window this morning where the world like a passer－by stops for a moment， nods to me and goes.

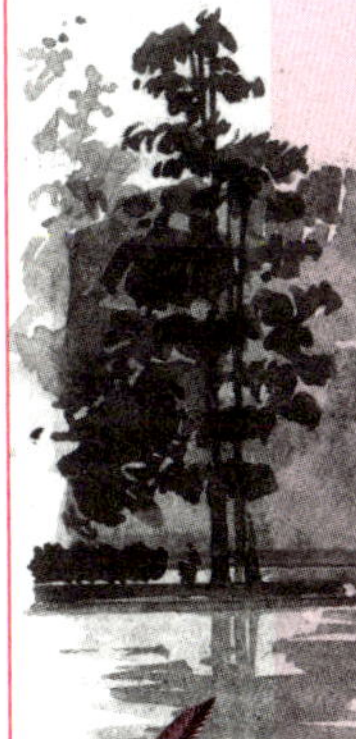

我今晨坐在窗前，世界如一个过路的人似的，停留了一会儿，向我点点头又走过去了。

17

There little thoughts are the rustle of leaves; they have their whisper of joy in my mind.

这些微思，是绿叶的簌簌之声呀；它们在我的心里，欢悦地微语着。

18

What you are you do not see，what you see is your shadow.

你看不见你自己，你所看见的只是你的影子。

19

My wishes are fools，they shout across thy song，my Master.

Let me but listen.

主呀，我的那些愿望真是愚傻呀，它们杂在你的歌声中喧叫着呢。

让我只是静听着吧。

20

I cannot choose the best.

The best chooses me.

我不能选择那最好的。

是那最好的选择我。

21

They throw their shadows before them who carry their lantern on their back.

那些把灯背在背上的人，把他们的影子投到了自己前面。

22

That I exist is a perpetual surprise which is life.

我的存在，对我是一个永久的神奇，这就是生活。

23

“We, the rustling leaves, have a voice that answers the storms, But who are you so silent?”

“I am a mere flower.”

“我们，萧萧的树叶，都有声响回答那暴风雨。但你是谁呢，那样地沉默着？”

“我不过是一朵花。”

24

Rest belongs to the work as the eyelids to the eyes.

休息隶属于工作，正如眼睑隶属于眼睛。

25

Man is a born child, his power is the power of growth.

人是一个初生的孩子，他的力量，就是生长的力量。

26

God expects answers for the flowers he sends us, not for the sun and the earth.

上帝希望我们酬答他的，在于他送给我们的花朵，而不在于太阳和土地。

27

The light that plays, like a naked child, among the green leaves happily knows not that man can lie.

光明如一个裸体的孩子，快快活活地在绿叶当中游戏，它不知道人是会欺诈的。

28

O Beauty, find thyself in love, not in the flattery of thy mirror.

啊，美呀，在爱中找你自己吧，不要到你镜子的谄谀中去找寻。

29

My heart beats her waves at the shore of the world and writes upon it her signature in tears with the words, “I love thee.”

我的心在世界的海岸上冲激着她的波浪，以热泪在上边写着她的题记：“我爱你。”

30

“Moon, for what do you wait?”

“To salute the sun for whom I must make way.”

“月儿呀，你在等候什么呢？”

"向我将让位给它的太阳致敬。"

31

The trees come up to my window like the yearning voice of the dumb earth.

绿树长到了我的窗前，仿佛是喑哑的大地发出的渴望的声音。

32

His own mornings are new surprises to God.

上帝自己的清晨，在他自己看来也是新奇的。

33

Life finds its wealth by the claims of the world, and its worth by the claims of love.

生命从世界得到它的资产，从爱情得到它的价值。

34

The dry river-bed finds no thanks for its past.

枯竭的河床，并不感谢它的过去。

35

The bird wishes it were a cloud.

The cloud wishes it were a bird.

鸟儿愿为一朵云。

云儿愿为一只鸟。

36

The waterfall sings, "I find my song, when I find my freedom."

瀑布歌道："我得到自由时便有歌声了。"

37

I cannot tell why this heart languishes in silence.

It is for small needs it never asks, or knows or

remembers.

我说不出这心为什么那样默默地颓丧着。

是为了它那不曾要求、不曾知道、不曾记得的小小需要。

38

Woman, when you move about in your household service your limbs sing like a hill stream among its pebbles.

妇人，你在料理家事的时候，你的手足歌唱着，正如山间的溪水歌唱着在小石中流过。

39

The sun goes to cross the Western sea, leaving its last salutation to the East.

当太阳横过西方的海面时，对着东方，留下他最后的敬礼。

40

Do not blame your food because you have no appetite.

不要因为你自己没有胃口而去责备你的食物。

41

The trees, like the longings of the earth, stand a tiptoe to peep at the heaven.

群树如表示大地的愿望似的，踮起脚，向天空窥望。

42

You smiled and talked to me of nothing and I felt that for this I had been waiting long.

你微微地笑着，不同我说什么话。而我觉得，为了这个，我已等待得久了。

43

The fish in the water is silent, the animal on the earth is noisy, the bird in the air is singing.

But Man has in him the silence of the sea, the noise of the earth and the music of the air.

水里的游鱼是沉默的，陆地上的兽类是喧闹的，空中的飞鸟是歌唱着的。

但是，人类却兼有海里的沉默、地上的喧闹与空中的音乐。

44

The world rushes on over the strings of the lingering heart making the music of sadness.

世界在踌躇之心的琴弦上跑过去，奏出忧郁的乐声。

45

He has made his weapons his gods.

When his weapons win he is defeated himself.

他把他的刀剑当作他的上帝。

当他的刀剑胜利时他自己却失败了。

46

God finds himself by creating.

神在创造中找到他自己。

47

Shadow, with her veil drawn, follows Light in secret meekness, with her silent steps of love.

阴影戴上她的面幕，秘密地，温顺地，用她的沉默的爱的脚步，跟在“光”后边。

48

The stars are not afraid to appear like fireflies.

群星不怕显得像萤火虫那样。

49

I thank thee that I am none of the wheels of power but I am one with the living creatures that are crushed by it.

谢谢上帝，我不是一个权力的轮子，而是被压在这轮下的活人之一。

50

The mind，sharp but not broad，sticks at every point but does not move.

心是尖锐的，不是宽博的，它执着在每一点上，却并不活动。

51

Your idol is shattered in the dust to prove that God's dust is greater than your idol.

你的偶像委散在尘土中了，这可证明上帝的尘土比你的偶像更伟大。

52

Man does not reveal himself in his history，he struggles up through it.

人不能在他的历史中表现出自己，他在历史中奋斗着露出头角。

53

While the glass lamp rebukes the earthen for calling it cousin，the moon rises，and the glass lamp，with a bland smile，calls her，

——My dear，dear sister.

玻璃灯因为瓦灯叫它作表兄而责备瓦灯，但明月出来时，玻璃灯却温和地微笑着，叫明月——“我亲爱的，亲爱的姐姐。”

54

Like the meeting of the seagulls and the waves we meet and come near.

The seagulls fly off，the waves roll away and we depart.

我们如海鸥之与波涛相遇似的，遇见了，走近了。

海鸥飞去，波涛滚滚地流开，我们也分别了。

55

My day is done, and I am like a boat drawn on the beach, listening to the dance-music of the tide in the evening.

我的白昼已经完了，于是我像一只泊在海滩上的小船，谛听着晚潮跳舞的乐声。

56

Life is given to us, we earn it by giving it.

我们的生命是天赋的，我们唯有献出生命，才能

得到生命。

57

We come nearest to the great when we are great in humility.

当我们是大为谦卑的时候，便是我们最接近伟大的时候。

58

The sparrow is sorry for the peacock at the burden of its tail.

麻雀看见孔雀负担着它的翎尾，替它担忧。

59

Never be afraid of the moments

——thus sings the voice of the everlasting.

决不要害怕刹那

——永恒之声这样唱着。

60

The hurricane seeks the shortest road by the no-road, and suddenly ends its search in the Nowhere.

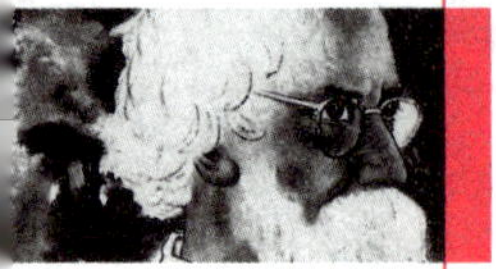

飓风于无路之中寻求最短之路，又突然在“无何有之国”终止了它的寻求。

61

Take my wine in my own cup，friend.

It loses its wreath of foam when poured into that of others.

在我自己的杯中，饮了我的酒吧，朋友。

一倒在别人的杯里，这酒的腾跃的泡沫便要消失了。

62

The Perfect decks itself in beauty for the love of the Imperfect.

“完全”为了对“不全”的爱，把自己装饰得美丽。

63

God says to man, "I heal you therefore I hurt, love you therefore punish."

上帝对人说道："我医治你，所以要伤害你，我爱你，所以要惩罚你。"

64

Thank the flame for its light, but do not forget the lampholder standing in the shade with constancy of patience.

谢谢火焰给你光明，但是不要忘了那执灯的人，他正坚忍地站在黑暗当中呢。

65

Tiny grass, your steps are small, but you possess the earth under your tread.

小草呀，你的足步虽小，但是你拥有足下的土地。

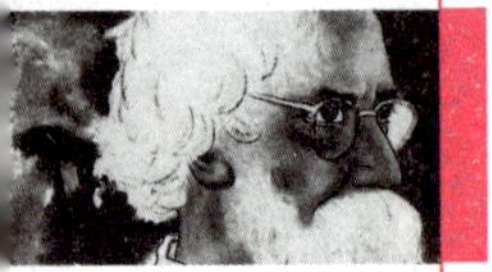

66

The infant flower opens its bud and cries, "Dear World, please do not fade."

幼花的蓓蕾开放了，它叫道："亲爱的世界呀，请不要萎谢了。"

67

God grows weary of great kingdoms, but never of little flowers.

上帝对于那些大帝国会感到厌恶，却决不会厌恶那些小小的花朵。

68

Wrong cannot afford defeat but Right can.

错误经不起失败，但是真理却不怕失败。

69

“I give my whole water in joy,” signs the waterfull, “though little of it is enough for the thirsty.”

瀑布歌唱道：“虽然渴者只要少许的水便够了，我却很快活地给与了我全部的水。”

70

Where is the fountain that throws up these flowers in a ceaseless outbreak of ecstasy?

把那些花朵抛掷上去的那一阵无休无止的狂欢大喜的劲儿，其源泉是在哪里呢？

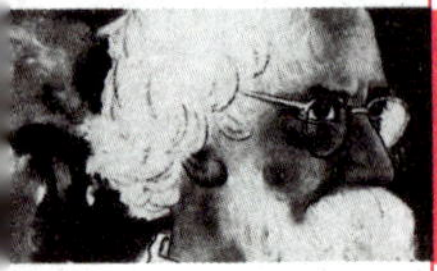

71

The woodcutter's axe begged for its handle from the tree.

The tree gave it.

樵夫的斧头，问树要斧柄。

树便给了它。

72

In my solitude of heart I feel the sigh of this widowed evening veiled with mist and rain.

这寡独的黄昏，沐着雾与雨，我在心的孤寂里，感觉到了它的叹息。

73

Chastity is a wealth that comes from abundance of love.

贞操是从丰富的爱情中生出来的财富。

74

The mist, like love, plays upon the heart of the hills and bring out surprises of beauty.

雾，像爱情一样，在山峰的心上游戏，生出种种美丽的变幻。

75

We read the world wrong and say that it deceives us.

我们把世界看错了，反说它欺骗我们。

76

The poet wind is out over the sea and the forest to seek his own voice.

诗人的风，正经过海洋和森林，追求它自己的歌声。

77

Every child comes with the message that God is not yet discouraged of man.

每一个孩子出生时都带来这样的启示：上帝对于人尚未灰心失望。

78

The grass seeks her crowd in the earth.

The tree seeks his solitude of the sky.

绿草求她地上的伴侣。

树木求他天空的寂寞。

79

Man barricades against himself.

人对他自己建筑起堤防来。

80

Your voice, my friend, wanders in my heart, like the muffled sound of the sea among these listening pines.

我的朋友，你的语声飘荡在我的心里，像那海水的低吟之声，缭绕在静听着的松林之间。

81

What is this unseen flame of darkness whose sparks are the stars?

这个不可见的黑暗之火焰，以繁星为其火花的，到底是什么呢？

82

Let life be beautiful like summer flowers and death like autumn leaves.

使生如夏花之绚烂，死如秋叶之静美。

83

He who wants to do good knocks at the gate；he who loves finds the gate open.

那想做好人的，在门外敲着门；那爱人的，看见门敞开着。

84

In death the many becomes one；in life the one becomes many.

Religion will be one when God is dead.

在死的时候，众多合而为一；在生的时候，一化为众多。

上帝死了的时候，宗教将合而为一。

85

The artist is the lover of Nature, therefore he is her slave and her master.

艺术家是自然的情人，所以他是自然的奴隶，也是自然的主人。

86

How far are you from me, O Fruit?

I am hidden in your heart, O Flower.

“你离我有多远呢，果实呀？”

“我藏在你心里呢，花呀。”

87

This longing is for the one who is felt in the dark, but not seen in the day.

这个渴望是为了那个在黑夜里感觉得到，在白天里却看不见的人。

88

“ You are the big drop of dew under the lotus leaf, I am the smaller one on its upper side. ” said the dewdrop to the lake.

露珠对湖水说道：“你是在荷叶下面的大露珠，我是在荷叶上面的较小的露珠。”

89

The scabbard is content to be dull when it protects the keenness of the sword.

刀鞘保护刀的锋利，它自己则满足于迟钝。

90

In darkness the One appears as uniform; in the light the One appears as manifold.

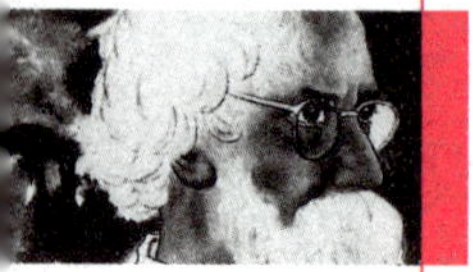

在黑暗中，“一”视若一体；在光亮中，“一”便视若众多。

91

The great earth makes herself hospitable with the help of the grass.

大地借助于绿草，显出她自己的殷勤好客。

92

The birth and death of the leaves are the rapid whirls of the eddy whose wider circles move slowly among stars.

绿叶的生与死乃是旋风的急骤的旋转，它更广大的旋转的圈子乃是在天上繁星之间徐缓的转动。

93

Power said to the world, “You are mine.”

The world kept it prisoner on her throne.

Love said to the world, "I am thine."

The world gave it the freedom of her house.

权势对世界说:"你是我的。"

世界便把权势囚禁在她的宝座下面。

爱情对世界说:"我是你的。"

世界便给予爱情在她屋内来往的自由。

94

The mist is like the earth's desire.

It hides the sun for whom she cries.

浓雾仿佛是大地的愿望。

它藏起了太阳，而太阳原是她所呼求的。

95

Be still, my heart, these great trees are prayers.

安静些吧，我的心，这些大树都是祈祷者呀。

96

The noise of the moment scoffs at the music of the Eternal.

瞬间的喧声，讥笑着永恒的音乐。

97

I think of other ages that floated upon the stream of life and love and death and are forgotten, and I feel the freedom of passing away.

我想起了浮泛在生与爱与死的川流上的许多别的时代，以及这些时代之被遗忘，我便感觉到离开尘世的自由了。

98

The sadness of my soul is her bride's veil.

It waits to be lifted in the night.

我灵魂里的忧郁就是她新婚的面纱。

这面纱等候着在夜间卸去。

99

Death's stamp gives value to the coin of life; making it possible to buy with life what is truly precious.

死之印记给生的钱币以价值，使它能够用生命

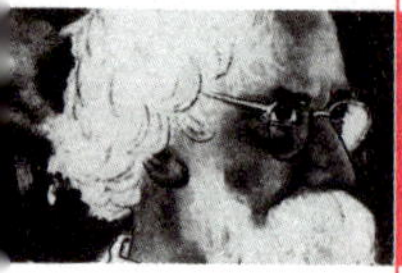

来购买那真正的宝物。

100

The cloud stood humbly in a corner of the sky.

The morning crowned it with splendour.

白云谦逊地站在天之一隅。

晨光给它戴上了霞彩。

101

The dust receives insult and in return offers her flowers.

尘土受到损辱，却以她的花朵来报答。

102

Do not linger to gather flowers to keep them，but walk on，for flowers will keep themselves blooming all your way.

只管走过去，不必逗留着去采了花朵来保存，因为一路上，花朵会继续开放的。

103

Roots are the branches down in the earth.

Branches are roots in the air.

根是地下的枝。

枝是空中的根。

104

The music of the far-away summer flutters around the Autumn seeking its former nest.

远远去了的夏之音乐，翱翔于秋间，寻求它的旧垒。

105

Do not insult your friend by lending him merits from your own pocket.

不要从你自己的袋里掏出勋绩借给你的朋友，这是在污辱他。

106

The touch of the nameless days clings to my heart like mosses round the old tree.

无名的日子的感触，攀缘在我的心上，正像那绿色的苔藓，攀缘在老树的周身。

107

The echo mocks her origin to prove she is the original.

回声嘲笑着她的原声，以证明她是原声。

108

God is ashamed when the prosperous boasts of his special favour.

当富贵利达的人夸说他得到上帝的特别恩惠时，上帝却羞了。

109

I cast my own shadow upon my path, because I have a lamp that has not been lighted.

我投射自己的影子在我的路上，因为我有一盏还没有点燃的明灯。

110

Man goes into the noisy crowed to drown his own clamour of silence.

人走进喧哗的群众里去，为的是要淹没自己沉默的呼号。

111

That which ends in exhaustion is death, but the perfect ending is in the endless.

终止于衰竭的是“死亡”，但“圆满”却终止于无穷。

112

The sun has his simple rode of light.

The clouds are decked with gorgeousness.

太阳只穿一件朴素的光衣，白云却披了灿烂的裙裾。

113

The hills are like shouts of children who raise their arms, trying to catch stars.

山峰如群儿之喧嚷，举起他们的双臂，想去捉天上的星星。

114

The road is lonely in its crowd for it is not loved.

道路虽然拥挤，却是寂寞的，因为它是不被爱的。

115

The power that boasts of its mischiefs is laughed at by the yellow leaves that fall, and clouds that pass by.

权势以它的恶行自夸，落下的黄叶与浮游的云片却在笑它。

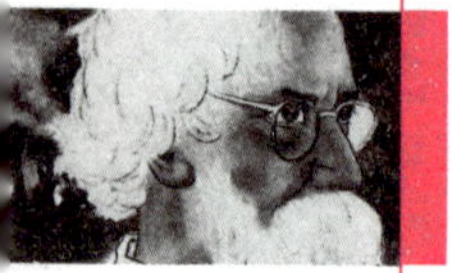

116

The earth hums to me today in the sun, like a woman at her spinning, some ballad of the ancient time in a forgotten tongue.

今天大地在阳光里向我营营哼鸣，像一个织着布的妇人，用一种已经被忘却的语言，哼着一些古代的歌曲。

117

The grass-blade is worthy of the great world where it grows.

绿草是无愧于它所生长的伟大世界的。

118

Dream is a wife who must talk,

Sleep is a husband who silently suffers.

梦是一个一定要谈话的妻子。

睡眠是一个默默忍受的丈夫。

119

The night kisses the fading day whispering to his ear, “I am death, your mother. I am to give you fresh birth.”

夜与逝去的日子接吻，轻轻地在他耳旁说道：“我是死，是你的母亲。我就要给你以新的生命。”

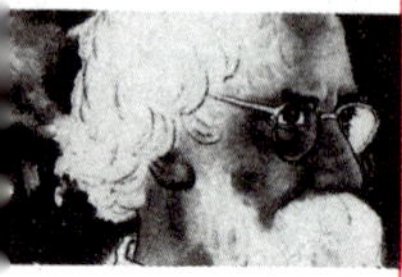

120

I feel thy beauty, dark night, like that of the loved woman when she has put out the lamp.

黑夜呀，我感觉到你的美了。你的美如一个可爱的妇人，当她把灯灭了的时候。

121

I carry in my world that flourishes the worlds that have failed.

我把在那些已逝去的世界上的繁荣带到我的世界来。

122

Dear friend, I feel the silence of your great thoughts of many a deepening eventide on this beach when I listen to these waves.

亲爱的朋友呀，当我静听着海涛时，我好几次在暮色深沉的黄昏里，在这个海岸上，感觉到你的伟大思想的沉默了。

123

The bird thinks it is an act of kindness to give the fish a life in the air.

鸟以为把鱼举在空中是一种慈善的举动。

124

"In the moon thou sendest thy love letters to me," said the night to the sun,

"I leave my answers in tears upon the grass."

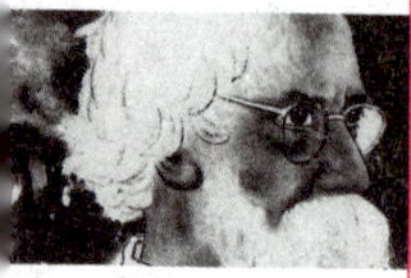

夜对太阳说道:“在月亮中,你送了你的情书给我。”

“我已在绿草上留下了我的流着泪点的回答了。”

125

The great is a born child; when he dies he gives his great childhood to the world.

伟人是一个天生的孩子，当他死时，他把他伟大的孩提时代给了世界。

126

Not hammer-strokes, but dance of the water sings the pebbles into perfection.

不是槌的打击，乃是水的载歌载舞，使鹅卵石臻于完美。

127

Bees sip honey from flowers and hum their thanks when they leave.

The gaudy butterfly is sure that the flowers owe thanks to him.

蜜蜂从花中啜蜜，离开时营营地道谢。

浮华的蝴蝶却相信花是应该向它道谢的。

128

To be outspoken is easy when you do not wait to speak the complete truth.

如果你不等待着要说出完全的真理，那么把话说出来是很容易的。

129

Asks the Possible to the Impossible,
Where is your dwelling-place?
In the dreams of the impotent, comes the answer.

“可能”问“不可能”道：
“你住在什么地方呢？”
它回答道：“在那无能为力者的梦境里。”

130

If you shut your door to all errors truth will be shut out.

如果你把所有的错误都关在门外，真理也要被关在外面了。

131

I hear some rustle of things behind my sadness of heart,

——I cannot see them.

我听见有些东西在我心的忧闷后面萧萧作响，

——我不能看见它们。

132

Leisure in its activity is work.

The stillness of the sea stirs in waves.

闲暇在动作时便是工作。

静止的海水荡动时便成波涛。

133

The leaf becomes flower when it loves.

The flower becomes fruit when it worships.

绿叶恋爱时便成了花。

花崇拜时便成了果实。

134

The roots below the earth claim no rewards for making the branches fruitful.

埋在地下的树根使树枝产生果实，却不要求什么报酬。

135

This rainy evening the wind is restless.

I look at the swaying branches and ponder over the greatness of all things.

阴雨的黄昏，风无休止地吹着。

我看着摇曳的树枝，感念万物的伟大。

136

Storm of midnight，like a giant child awakened in the untimely dark，has begun to play and shout.

子夜的风雨，如一个巨大的孩子，在不合时宜的黑夜里醒来，开始游戏和喧闹。

137

Thou raisest thy waves vainly to follow thy lover，O sea，thou lonely bride of the storm.

海呀，你这暴风雨的孤寂的新妇呀，你虽掀起波浪追随你的情人，但是无用呀。

138

“I am ashamed of my emptiness. ” said the Word to the Work.

“I know how poor I am when I see you.” said the Work to the Word.

文字对工作说道：“我惭愧我的空虚。”

工作对文字说道：“当我看见你时，我便知道我是怎样的贫乏了。”

139

Time is the wealth of change，but the clock in its parody makes it mere change and no wealth.

时间是变化的财富，时钟模仿它，却只有变化而没有财富。

140

Truth in her dress finds facts too tight.

In fiction she moves with ease.

真理穿了衣裳，觉得事实太拘束了。

在想象中，她却转动得很舒畅。

141

When I travelled to here and to there, I was tired of thee, O Road, but now when thou leadest me to everywhere I am wedded to thee in love.

当我到这里或那里旅行时，路呀，我厌倦你了；但是现在，当你引导我到各处去时，我便爱上你，与你结婚了。

142

Let me think that there is one among those stars that guides my life through the dark unknown.

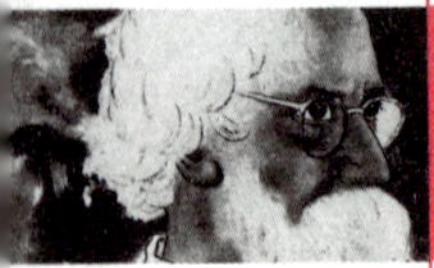

让我设想，在群星之中，有一颗星是指导着我的生命通过不可知的黑暗的。

143

Woman, with the grace of your fingers you touched my things and order came out like music.

妇人，你用了你美丽的手指，触着我的什物，秩序便如音乐似的生出来了。

144

One sad voice has its nest among the ruins of the years.

It sings to me in the night,

——I loved you.

一个忧郁的声音，筑巢于似水年华中。

它在夜里向我唱道：

——“我爱你。”

145

The flaming fire warns me off by its own glow.

Save me from the dying embers hidden under ashes.

燃着的火，以它熊熊之光焰警告我不要走近它。

把我从潜藏在灰中的余烬里救出来吧。

146

I have my stars in the sky.

But oh for my little lamp unlit in my house.

我有群星在天上，

但是，唉，我屋里的小灯却没有点亮。

147

The dust of the dead words clings to thee.

Wash thy soul with silence.

死文字的尘土沾着你。

用沉默去洗净你的灵魂吧。

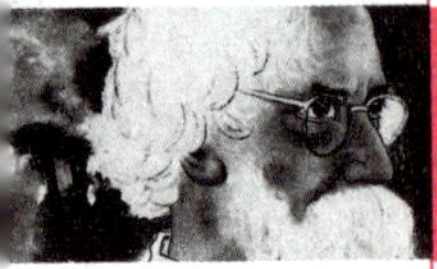

148

Gaps are left in life through which comes the sad music of death.

生命里留了许多罅隙，从中传来了死亡的忧郁的音乐。

149

The world has opened its heart of light in the morning.

Come out，my heart，with thy love to meet it.

世界已在早晨敞开了它的光明之心。

出来吧，我的心，带着你的爱去与它相会。

150

My thoughts shimmer with these shimmering leaves and my heart sings with the touch of this sunlight; my life is glad to be floating with all things into the blue of space, into the dark of time.

我的思想随着这些闪耀的绿叶而闪耀着，我的心灵因了这日光的抚摸而歌唱；我的生命因为偕了万物一同浮泛在空间的蔚蓝、时间的墨黑中而感到欢快。

151

God's great power is in the gentle breeze, not in the storm.

上帝的巨大威权是在柔和的微风里，而不在狂风暴雨之中。

152

This is a dream in which things are all loose and they oppress.

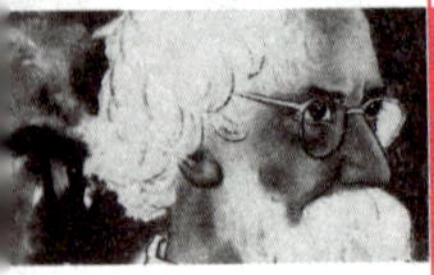

I shall find them gathered in thee when I awake and shall be free.

在梦中，一切事都散漫着，都压着我，但这不过是一个梦呀。当我醒来时，我将觉得这些事都已聚集在你那里，我也便将自由了。

153

“Who is there to take up my duties? ” asked the setting sun.

“I shall do what I can, my Master. ” said the earthen lamp.

落日问道：“有谁继续我的职责呢？”

瓦灯说道：“我将会尽我所能地做去，我的主人。”

154

By plucking her petals you do not gather the beauty of the flower.

采着花瓣时，得不到花的美丽。

155

Silence will carry your voice like the nest that holds the sleeping birds.

沉默蕴蓄着语声，正如鸟巢拥围着睡鸟。

156

The Great walks with the Small without fear.

The Middling keeps aloof.

大的不怕与小的同游。

居中的却避而远之。

157

The night opens the flowers in secret and allows the day to get thanks.

夜秘密地把花开放了，却让白日去领受谢辞。

158

Power takes as ingratitude the writhings of its victims.

权势认为牺牲者的痛苦是忘恩负义。

159

When we rejoice in our fulness，then we can part with our fruits with joy.

当我们以我们的充实为乐时，那么，我们便能很快乐地跟我们的果实分手了。

160

The raindrops kissed the earth and whispered,

——“We are thy homesick children, mother, come back to thee from the heaven.”

雨点吻着大地，微语道：

——“我们是你的思家的孩子，母亲，现在从天上回到你这里来了。”

161

The cobweb pretends to catch dewdrops and catches flies.

蛛网好像要捉露点，却捉住了苍蝇。

162

Love! When you come with the burning lamp of pain in your hand, I can see your face and know you as bliss.

爱情呀，当你手拿着点亮了的痛苦之灯走来时，我能够看见你的脸，而且以你为幸福。

163

"The leaned say that your lights will one day be no more." said the firefly to the stars.

The stars made no answer.

萤火对天上的星说道：

"学者说你的光明总有一天会消灭的。"

天上的星不回答它。

164

In the dusk of the evening the bird of some early dawn comes to the nest of my silence.

在黄昏的微光里，有那清晨的鸟儿来到了我沉默的鸟巢里。

165

Thoughts pass in my mind like flocks of ducks in the sky.

I hear the voice of their wings.

思想掠过我的心上，如一群野鸭飞过天空。

我听见它们的鼓翼之声了。

166

The canal loves to think that rivers exist solely to supply it with water.

沟洫总喜欢想：河流的存在，是专为它供给水流的。

167

The world has kissed my soul with its pain, asking for its return in songs.

世界以它的痛苦同我接吻，而要求歌声做报酬。

168

That which oppresses me，is it my soul trying to come out in the open，or the soul of the world knocking at my heart for its entrance?

压迫着我的，到底是我的想要外出的灵魂呢，还是那世界的灵魂，敲着我的心门，想要进来呢?

169

Thought feeds itself with its own words and grows.

思想以自己的言语喂养自己，从而成长起来。

170

I have dipped the vessel of my heart into this silent hour；it has filled with love.

我把我的心之碗轻轻浸入这沉默时刻中，它充满了爱了。

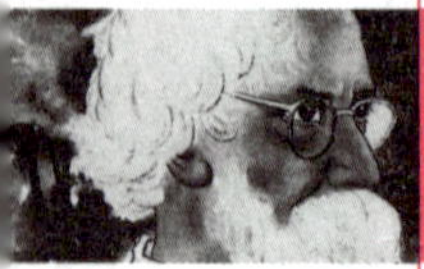

171

Either you have work or you have not.

When you have to say, “Let us do something”, then begins mischief.

或者你在工作，或者你没有。

当你不得不说：“让我们做些事吧！”那么就要开始胡闹了。

172

The sunflower blushed to own the nameless flower as her kin.

The sun rose and smiled on it, saying, "Are you well, my darling?"

向日葵羞于把无名的花朵看作它的同胞。

太阳升上来了，向它微笑，说道："你好么，我的宝贝儿？"

173

"Who drives me forward like fate?"

"The Myself striding on my back."

"谁如命运似的推着我向前走呢？"

"那是我自己，在身后大跨步走着。"

174

The clouds fill the watercups of the river, hiding themselves in the distant hills.

云把水倒在河的水杯里，它们自己却藏在远山之中。

175

I spill water from my water jar as I walk on my way, very little remains for my home.

我一路走去，从我的水瓶中漏出水来，只剩下极少极少的水供我家里使用了。

176

The water in a vessel is sparkling; the water in the sea is dark.

The small truth has words that are clear; the great truth has great silence.

杯中的水是光辉的；海中的水却是黑色的。

小理可以用文字来说清楚；大理却只有沉默。

177

Your smile was the flowers of your own fields, your talk was the rustle of your own mountain pines, but your heart was the woman that we all know.

你的微笑是你自己田园里的花，你的谈吐是你自己山上的松林的萧萧；但是你的心呀，却是那个女人，那个我们全都认识的女人。

178

It is the little things that I leave behind for my loved ones——great things are for everyone.

我把小小的礼物留给我所爱的人——大的礼物却留给众生。

179

Woman, thou hast encircled the world's heart with the depth of thy tears as the sea has the earth.

妇人呀，你用眼泪的深邃包绕着世界的心，正如大海包绕着大地。

180

The sunshine greets me with a smile.

The rain, his sad sister, talks to my heart.

太阳以微笑向我问候。

雨，他的忧闷的姐姐，和我的心谈话。

181

My flower of the day dropped its petals forgotten.

In the evening it ripens into a golden fruit of memory.

我的昼间之花，落下它那被遗忘的花瓣。

在黄昏中，这花成熟为一颗记忆的金果。

182

I am like the road in the night listening to the footfalls of its memories in silence.

我像那夜间之路，正静悄悄地听着记忆的足音。

183

The evening sky to me is like a window，and a lighted lamp，and a waiting behind it.

黄昏的天空，在我看来，像一扇窗户，一盏灯火，灯火背后的一次等待。

184

He who is too busy doing good finds no time to be good.

太急于做好事的人，反而找不到时间去做好人。

185

I am the autumn cloud, empty of rain, see my fulness in the field of ripened rice.

我是秋云，空空地不载着雨水，但在成熟的稻田中，可以看见我的充实。

186

They hated and killed and men praised them.

But God in shame hastens to hide its memory under the green grass.

他们嫉妒，他们残杀，人反而称赞他们。

然而上帝却害了羞，匆匆地把他的记忆埋藏在绿草下面。

187

Toes are the fingers that have forsaken their past.

脚趾乃是舍弃了其过去的手指。

188

Darkness travels towards light, but blindness towards death.

黑暗向光明旅行，但是盲者却向死亡旅行。

189

The pet dog suspects the universe for scheming to take its place.

小狗疑心大宇宙阴谋篡夺它的位置。

190

Sit still, my heart, do not raise your dust.

Let the world find its way to you.

静静地坐着吧，我的心，不要扬起你的尘土。

让世界自己寻路向你走来。

191

The bow whispers to the arrow before it speeds forth,

"Your freedom is mine."

弓在箭要射出之前，低声对箭说道：

“你的自由是我的。”

192

Woman, in your laughter you have the music of the fountain of life.

妇人，在你的笑声里有着生命之泉的音乐。

193

A mind all logic is like a knife all blade.

It makes the hand bleed that uses it.

全是理智的心，恰如一柄全是锋刃的刀。

叫使用它的人手上流血。

194

God loves man's lamplight better than his own great stars.

上帝爱人间的灯光甚于他自己的群星。

195

This world is the world of wild storms kept tame with the music of beauty.

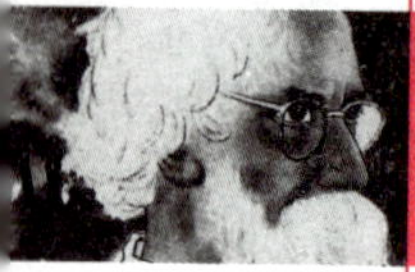

这世界乃是为美丽的音乐所驯服了的、狂风骤雨的世界。

196

“My heart is like the golden casket of thy kiss.” said the sunset cloud to the sun.

晚霞向太阳说道：

“我的心经了你的吻，便似金的宝箱了。”

197

By touching you may kill，by keeping away you may possess.

接触着，你也许会杀害；远离着，你也许会占有。

198

The cricket's chirp and the patter of rain come to me through the dark，like the rustle of dreams from my past youth.

蟋蟀的唧唧，夜雨的淅沥，从黑暗中传到我的耳边，好似我已逝的少年时代沙沙地来到我梦境中。

199

“I have lost my dewdrop,” cries the flower to the morning sky that has lost all its stars.

花朵向落尽了它所有的星辰的曙天叫道：“我的露珠全失落了。”

200

The burning log bursts in flame and cries,
“This is my flower, my death.”

燃烧着的木块，熊熊地生出火光，叫道：
“这是我的花朵，我的死亡。”

201

The wasp thinks that the honeyhive of the neighboring bees is too small.

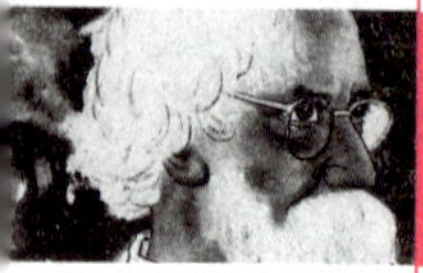

His neighbors ask him to build one still smaller.

黄蜂认为邻居蜜蜂的储蜜之巢太小。

他的邻人要他去建筑一个更小的。

202

“I cannot keep your waves，” says the bank to the river，“let me keep your footprints in my heart.”

河岸向河流说道：“我不能留住你的波浪。让我保存你的足印在我的心里吧。”

203

The day, with the noise of this little earth, drowns the silence of all worlds.

白日以这小小地球的喧扰，淹没了整个宇宙的沉默。

204

The song feels the infinite in the air, the picture in the earth, the poem in the air and the earth; for its words have meaning that walks and music that soars.

歌声在天空中感到无限，图画在地上感到无限，诗呢，无论在空中，在地上都是如此；因为诗的词句含有能走动的意义与能飞翔的音乐。

205

When the sun goes down to the West, the East of his morning stands before him in silence.

太阳在西方落下时，他的早晨的东方已静悄悄地站在它面前。

206

Let me not put myself wrongly to my world and set it against me.

让我不要错误地把自己放在我的世界里而使它

反对我。

207

Praise shames me, for I secretly beg for it.

荣誉使我感到惭愧，因为我暗地里求着它。

208

Let my doing nothing when I have nothing to do become untroubled in its depth of peace like the evening in the seashore when the water is silent.

当我没有什么事做时，便让我不做什么事，不受骚扰地沉入安静深处吧，一如那海水沉默时海边的暮色。

209

Maiden, your simplicity, like the blueness of the lake, reveals your depth of truth.

少女呀，你的纯朴，如湖水之碧，表现出你的

真理的深邃。

210

The best does not come alone.

It comes with the company of the all.

最好的东西不是独来的，

它伴了所有的东西同来。

211

God's right hand is gentle, but terrible is his left hand.

上帝的右手是慈爱的，但是他的左手却可怕。

212

My evening came among the alien trees and spoke in a language which my morning stars did not know.

我的晚色从陌生的树木中走来，它用我的晨星所不懂得的语言说话。

213

Night's darkness is a bag that bursts with the gold of the dawn.

夜之黑暗是一只口袋，迸发出黎明的金光。

214

Our desire lends the colors of the rainbow to the mere mists and vapours of life.

我们的欲望把彩虹的颜色借给那只不过是云雾的人生。

215

God waits to win back his own flowers as gifts from man's hands.

上帝等待着，要从人的手上把他自己的花朵作为礼物赢回去。

216

My sad thoughts tease me asking me their own names.

我的忧思缠绕着我，要问我它们自己的名字。

217

The service of the fruit is precious, the service of the flower is sweet, but let my service be the service of the leaves in its shade of humble devotion.

果实的事业是尊贵的，花的事业是甜美的；但是让我做叶的事业吧，叶是谦逊地、专心地垂着绿荫的。

218

My heart has spread its sails to the idle winds for the shadowy island of anywhere.

我的心向着阑珊的风张了帆，要到无论何处的荫凉之岛去。

219

Men are cruel, but Man is kind.

独夫们是凶暴的，但人民是善良的。

220

Make me thy cup and let my fulness be for thee and for thine.

把我当作你的杯吧，让我为了你，而且为了你的人而盛满了水吧。

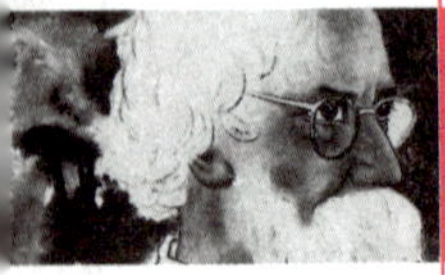

221

The storm is like the cry of some god in pain whose love the earth refuses.

狂风暴雨像是那因他的爱情被大地拒绝而在痛苦中的天神的哭声。

222

The world does not leak because death is not a crack.

世界不会裂开，因为死亡并不是一个罅隙。

223

Life has become richer by the love that has been lost.

生命因为付出了的爱情而更为富足。

224

My friend，your great heart shone with the sunrise of the East，Like the snowy summit of a lonely hill in the dawn.

我的朋友，你伟大的心闪射出东方朝阳的光芒，正如黎明中一个积雪的孤峰。

225

The fountain of death makes the still water of life play.

死之流泉，使生的止水跳跃。

226

Those who have everything but thee, my God, laugh at those who have nothing but thyself.

那些有一切东西而没有您的人，我的上帝，在讥笑着那些没有别的东西而只有您的人呢。

227

The movement of life has its rest in its own music.

生命的运动在它自己的音乐里得到休息。

228

Kicks only raise dust and not crops from the earth.

踢足只能从地上扬起尘土而不能得到收获。

229

Our names are the light that glows on the sea waves at night and then dies without leaving its signature.

107

我们的名字，便是夜里海波上发出的光，痕迹也不留就泯灭了。

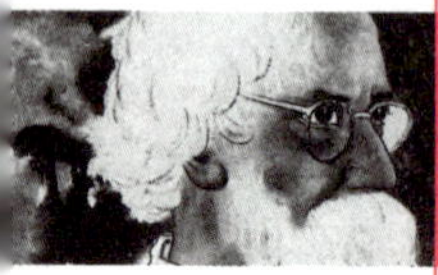

230

Let him only see the thorns who has eyes to see the rose.

让睁眼看着玫瑰花的人也看看它的刺。

231

Set the bird's wings with gold and it will never again soar in the sky.

鸟翼系上了黄金，这鸟便永不能再在天上翱翔了。

232

The same lotus of our clime blooms here in the alien water with the same sweetness, under another name.

我们地方的荷花又在这陌生的水上开了花，放出同样的清香，只是名字换了。

233

In heart's perspective the distance looms large.

在心的远景里，那相隔的距离显得更广阔了。

234

The moon has her light all over the sky, her dark spots to herself.

月儿把她的光明遍照在天上，却留着她的黑斑给自己。

235

Do not say, "It is morning," and dismiss it with a mane of yesterday.

See it for the first time as a new-born child that has no name.

不要说"这是早晨"，别用一个"昨天"的名词把它打发掉。把它当作你第一次看到的还没有名字的新生儿吧。

236

Smoke boasts to the sky, and Ashes to the earth, that they are brothers to the fire.

青烟对天空夸口，灰烬对大地夸口，都以为它们是火的兄弟。

237

The raindrop whispered to the jasmine, "Keep me in your heart forever."

The jasmine sighed, "Alas", and dropped to the

ground.

雨点向茉莉花微语道："把我永久地留在你的心里吧。"

茉莉花叹息了一声，落在地上了。

238

Timid thoughts, do not be afraid of me.

I am a poet.

腆怯的思想呀，不要怕我。

我是一个诗人。

239

The dim silence of my mind seems filled with crickets' chirp

——the grey twilight of sound.

我的心在朦胧的沉默里，似乎充满了蟋蟀的鸣声

——那灰色的微明的歌声。

240

Rockets, your insult to the stars follows yourself back to the earth.

爆竹呀，你对群星的侮蔑，又跟着你自己回到地上来了。

241

Thou hast led me through my crowded travels of the day to my evening's loneliness.

I wait for its meaning through the stillness of the night.

您曾经带领着我，穿过我白天的拥挤不堪的旅程，到达了我的黄昏孤寂之境。

在通宵的寂静里，我等待着它的意义。

242

This life is the crossing of a sea，where we meet in the same narrow ship.

In death we reach the shore and go to our different worlds.

我们的生命就像渡过一个大海，我们都相聚在这个狭小的舟中。

死时，我们便到了岸，各往各的世界去了。

243

The stream of truth flows through its channels of mistakes.

真理之川从它的错误的沟渠中流过。

244

My heart is homesick today for the one sweet hour across the sea of time.

今天我的心是在想家了，在想着那跨过时间之海的那一个甜蜜的时候。

245

The bird-song is the echo of the morning light back from the earth.

鸟的歌声是曙光从大地反响过去的回声。

246

"Are you too proud to kiss me? " the morning light asks the buttercup.

晨光问毛茛道：“你是骄傲得不肯和我接吻么？”

247

“How may I sing to thee and worship, O Sun？” asked the little flower.

“By the simple silence of thy purity，” answered the sun.

小花问道：“我要怎样地对你唱，怎样地崇拜你呢，太阳呀？”

太阳答道：“只要用你纯洁的简朴的沉默。”

248

Man is worse than an animal when he is an animal.

当人是兽时，他比兽还坏。

249

Dark clouds become heaven's flowers when kissed by light.

黑云受光的接吻时便变成天上的花朵。

250

Let not the sword-blade mock its handle for being blunt.

不要让刀锋讥笑它柄子的拙钝。

251

The night's silence, like a deep lamp, is burning with the light of its milky way.

夜的沉默，如一个深深的灯盏，银河便是它燃着的灯光。

252

Around the sunny island of life swells day and night death's limitless song of the sea.

死像大海的无限的歌声，日夜冲击着生命的光明岛的四周。

253

Is not this mountain like a flower, with its petals of hill, drinking the sunlight?

花瓣似的山峰在饮着日光，这山岂不像一朵花吗？

254

The real with its meaning read wrong and emphasis misplaced is the unreal.

“真实”的含义被误解，轻重被倒置，那就成了“不真实”。

255

Find your beauty, my heart, from the world's movement, like the boat that has the grace of the wind and the water.

我的心呀，从世界的流动找你的美吧，正如那

小船得到风与水的优美似的。

256

The eyes are not proud of their sight but of their eyeglasses.

眼不能以视来骄人，却以它们的眼镜来骄人。

257

I live in this little world of mine and am afraid to make it the least less. Lift me into thy world and let me have the freedom gladly to lose my all.

我住在我这个小小的世界里，生怕使它再缩小一丁点儿。把我抬举到您的世界里去吧，让我高高兴兴地失去我的一切自由。

258

The false can never grow into truth by growing in power.

虚伪永远不能凭借它生长在权力中而变成真实。

259

My heart, with its lapping waves of song, longs to caress this green world of the sunny day.

我的心，同着它的歌的拍子拍舐岸的波浪，渴望着要抚爱这个阳光熙和的绿色世界。

260

Wayside grass, love the star, then your dreams will come out in flowers.

道旁的草，爱那天上的星吧，你的梦境便可在花朵里实现了。

261

Let your music, like a sword, pierce the noise of the market to its heart.

让你的音乐如一柄利刃，直刺入市井喧扰的心中吧。

262

The trembling leaves of this tree touch my heart like the fingers of an infant child.

这树的颤动之叶，触动着我的心，像一个婴儿的手指。

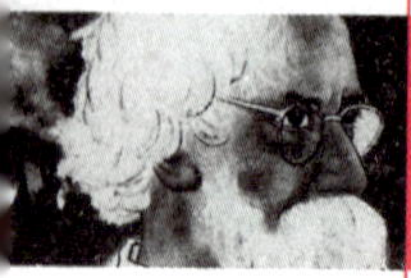

263

The little flower lies in the dust.

It sought the path of the butterfly.

小花睡在尘土里。

它寻求蛱蝶走的道路。

264

I am in the world of the roads.

The night comes. Open thy gate, thou world of the home.

我是在道路纵横的世界上。

夜来了。打开您的门吧，家之世界啊！

265

I have sung the songs of thy day.

In the evening let me carry thy lamp through the stormy path.

我已经唱过了您的白天的歌。

在黄昏的时候，让我拿着您的灯走过风雨飘摇的道路吧。

266

I do not ask thee into the house.

Come into my infinite loneliness，my Lover.

我不要求你进我的屋里。

你且到我无量的孤寂中来吧，我的爱人！

267

Death belongs to life as birth does.

The walk is in the raising of the foot as in the laying of it down.

死亡隶属于生命，正如出生一样。

举足是在走路，正如落足也是在走路。

268

I have learnt the simple meaning of thy whispers in flowers and sunshine——teach me to know thy words in pain and death.

我已经学会了你在花与阳光里微语的意义——再教我明白你在苦与死中所说的话吧。

269

The night's flower was late when the morning kissed her，she shivered and sighed and dropped to the ground.

夜的花朵来晚了，当早晨吻着她时，她颤栗着，叹息了一声，萎落在地上。

270

Through the sadness of all things I hear the crooning of the Eternal Mother.

从万物的愁苦中，我听见了“永恒母亲”的呻吟。

271

I came to your shore as a stranger, I lived in your house as a guest, I leave your door as a friend, my earth.

大地呀，我到你岸上时是一个陌生人，住在你屋内时是一个宾客，离开你的门时是一个朋友。

272

Let my thoughts come to you, when I am gone, like the after glow of sunset at the margin of starry silence.

当我离开时，让我的思想到你那里去，如那夕阳的余光，映在沉默的星天的边上。

273

Light in my heart the evening star of rest and then let the night whisper to me of love.

在我的心头燃点起那休憩的黄昏星吧，然后让黑夜向我微语着爱情。

274

I am a child in the dark.

I stretch my hands through the coverlet of night for thee，Mother.

我是一个在黑暗中的孩子。

我从夜的被单里向您伸出我的双手，母亲。

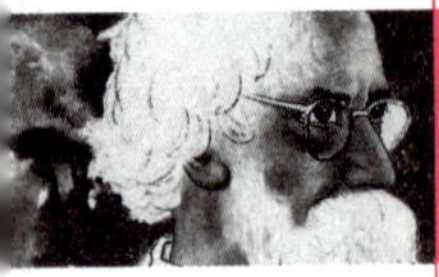

275

The day of work is done. Hide my face in your arms, Mother.

Let me dream.

白天的工作做完了。

把我的脸掩藏在您的臂间吧，母亲。让我入梦吧。

276

The lamp of meeting burns long; it goes out in a moment at the parting.

集会时的灯光，点了很久；会散时，灯便立刻灭了。

277

One word keeps for me in thy silence, O World, when I am dead, “I have loved”.

当我死时，世界呀，请在你的沉默中，替我留着“我已经爱过了”这句话吧。

278

We live in this world when we love it.

当我们热爱这世界时，我们便生活在这世界上。

279

Let the dead have the immortality of fame, but the living the immortality of love.

让死者有那不朽的名，但让生者有那不朽的爱。

280

I have seen thee as the half-awakened child sees his mother in the dusk of the dawn and then smiles and sleeps again.

我看见你，像那半醒的婴孩在黎明的微光里看见他的母亲，于是又微笑着睡去了。

281

I shall die again and again to know that life is inexhaustible.

我将死了又死，以明白生是无穷无尽的。

282

While I was passing with the crowd in the road I saw thy smile from the balcony and I sang and forgot all noise.

当我和拥挤的人群一同在路上走过时，看见您从阳台上送来的微笑，我歌唱着，忘却了所有的喧哗。

283

Love is life in its fulness like the cup with its wine.

爱就是充实了的生命，正如盛满了酒的酒杯。

284

They light their own lamps and sing their own words in their temples.

But the birds sing thy name in thine own morning light,

—— for thy name is joy.

他们点了自己的灯，在他们的寺院内，吟唱他们的话语。

但是小鸟们却在你的晨光中，唱着你的名字——因为你的名字便是快乐。

285

Lead me in the centre of thy silence to fill my heart with songs.

领我到您的沉寂的中心，使我的心充满了歌吧。

286

Let them live who choose in their own hissing world of fireworks.

My heart longs for thy stars, my God.

让那些选择了自己焰火嗞嗞的世界的人，生活在那里吧。

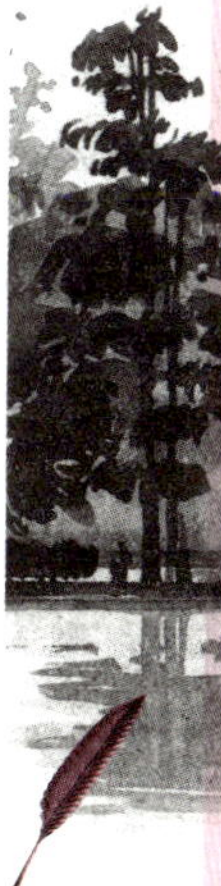

我的心渴望着您的繁星，我的上帝。

287

Love's pain sang round my life like the unplumbed sea, and love's joy sang like birds in its flowering groves.

爱的痛苦环绕着我的一生，像汹涌的大海似的唱着；而爱的快乐却像鸟儿们在花林里似的唱着。

288

Put out the lamp when thou wishest.

I shall know thy darkness and shall love it.

假如您愿意，您就熄了灯吧。

我将明白您的黑暗，而且将喜爱它。

289

When I stand before thee at the days end thou shalt see my scars and know that I had my wounds and also my healing.

当我在那日子的终了，站在您的面前时，您将看见我的伤疤，而知道我有许多创伤，但也有医治的法儿。

290

Some day I shall sing to thee in the sunrise of some other world, “I have seen thee before in the light of the earth, in the love of man.”

总有一天，我要在别的世界的晨光里对你唱道：“我以前在地球的光里，在人的爱里，已经见过你了。”

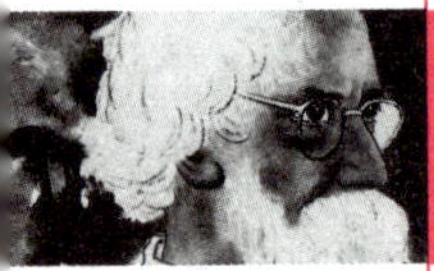

291

Clouds come floating into my life from other days no longer to shed rain or usher storm but to give colour to my sunset sky.

从别的日子里飘浮到我的生命里的黑云，不再落下雨点或引起风暴了，却只给予我的夕阳的天空以色彩。

292

Truth raises against itself the storm that scatters its seeds broadcast.

真理引起了反对它自己的狂风骤雨，那场风雨吹散了真理的广播的种子。

293

The storm of the last night has crowned this morning with golden peace.

昨夜的风雨给今日的早晨戴上了金色的和平。

294

Truth seems to come with its final word; and the final word gives birth to its next.

真理仿佛带了它的结论而来；而那结论却产生了它的第二个。

295

Blessed is he whose fame does not outshine his truth.

他是有福的，因为他的名望并没有比他的真实更光亮。

296

Sweetness of thy name fills my heart when I forget mine——like thy morning sun when the mist is melted.

您的名字的甜蜜充溢着我的心，而我忘掉了我

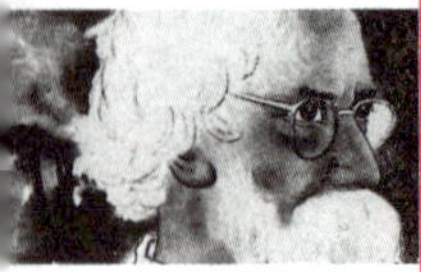

自己的——就像您的早晨的太阳升起时，那大雾便消失了。

297

The silent night has the beauty of the mother and the clamorous day of the child.

静悄悄的黑夜具有母亲的美丽，而吵闹的白天具有孩子的美丽。

298

The world loved man when he smiled. The world became afraid of him when he laughed.

当人微笑时，世界爱了他；但他大笑时，世界便怕他了。

299

God waits for man to regain his childhood in wisdom.

上帝等待着人在智慧中重新获得童年。

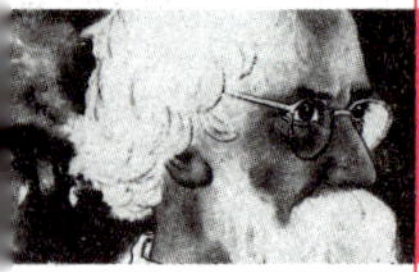

300

Let me feel this world as thy love taking form, then my love will help it.

让我感到这个世界乃是您的爱的成形吧，那么，我的爱也将帮助着它。

301

Thy sunshine smiles upon the winter days of my heart, never doubting of its spring flowers.

您的阳光对着我心头的冬天微笑着，从来不怀疑它春天的花朵。

302

God kisses the finite in his love and man the infinite.

上帝在他的爱里吻着“有涯”，而人却吻着“无涯”。

303

Thou crossest desert lands of barren years to reach the moment of fulfilment.

您越过不毛之年的沙漠而到达了圆满的时刻。

304

God's silence ripens man's thoughts into speech.

上帝的静默使人的思想成熟为语言。

305

Thou wilt find, Eternal Traveller, marks of thy footsteps across my songs.

“永恒的旅客”呀，你可以在我的歌中找到你的足迹。

306

Let me not shame thee, Father, who displayest thy glory in thy children.

让我不至羞辱您吧，父亲，您在您的孩子们身上显现出您的光荣。

307

Cheerless is the day, the light under frowning clouds is like a punished child with traces of tears on its pale

cheeks, and the cry of the wind is like the cry of a wounded world. But I know I am traveling to meet my friend.

这一天是不快活的。光在蹙额的云下，如一个被责打的儿童，在灰白的脸上留着泪痕；风又号叫着，似一个受伤的世界的哭声。但是我知道，我正跋涉着去会我的朋友。

308

Tonight there is a stir among the palm leaves, a swell in the sea, full Moon, like the heart-throb of the world. From what unknown sky hast thou carried in thy silence the aching secret of love?

今天晚上棕榈叶在嚓嚓地作响，海上有大浪，满月啊，就像世界在心脉悸跳。从什么不可知的天空，您在您的沉默里带来了爱的痛苦的秘密？

309

I dream of a star, an island of light, where I shall be born and in the depth of its quickening leisure my life will ripen its works like the rice-field in the autumn sun.

我梦见一颗星，一个光明的岛屿，我将在那里出生。在它快速的闲暇深处，我的生命将成熟它的事业，像在秋天的阳光之下的稻田。

310

The smell of the wet earth in the rain rises like a great chant of praise from the voiceless multitude of the insignificant.

雨中的湿土的气息，就像从渺小的无声的群众那里传来的一阵巨大的赞美歌声。

311

That love can ever lose is a fact that we cannot accept as truth.

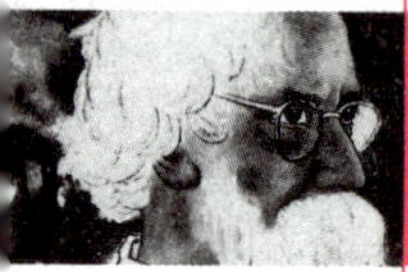

说爱情会失去的那句话，是我们不能够当作真理来接受的一个事实。

312

We shall know some day that death can never rob us of that which our soul has gained, for her gains are one with herself.

我们总有一天会明白，死永远不能够夺去我们的灵魂所获得的东西。因为她所获得的，和她自己是一体。

313

God comes to me in the dusk of my evening with the flowers from my past kept fresh in his basket.

上帝在我的黄昏的微光中，带着花来到我这里。这些花都是我过去之时的，在他的花篮中还保存得很新鲜。

314

When all the strings of my life will be tuned, my Master, then at every touch of thine will come out the music of love.

主呀，当我的生之琴弦都已调得和谐时，你的一弹一奏，都可以发出爱的乐声来。

315

Let me live truly, my Lord, so that death to me become true.

让我真真实实地活着吧，我的上帝。这样，死对于我也就成了真实的了。

316

Man's history is waiting in patience for the triumph of the insulted man.

人类的历史在很忍耐地等待着被侮辱者的胜利。

317

I feel thy gaze upon my heart this moment like the sunny silence of the morning upon the lonely field whose harvest is over.

我这一刻感到你的眼光正落在我的心上，像那早晨阳光中的沉默落在已收获的孤寂的田野上一样。

318

I long for the Island of Songs across this heaving Sea of Shouts.

在这喧哗的波涛起伏的海中，我渴望着咏歌之岛。

319

The prelude of the night is commenced in the music of the sunset, in its solemn hymn to the ineffable dark.

夜的序曲开始于夕阳西下的音乐，开始于它向难以形容的黑暗所作的庄严赞歌。

320

I have scaled the peak and found no shelter in fame's bleak and barren height.

Lead me, my Guide, before the light fades, into the valley of quiet where life's harvest mellows into golden wisdom.

我攀登上高峰，发现在名誉的荒芜不毛的高处，简直找不到一个遮身之地。

我的引导者啊，领着我在光明逝去之前，进到沉静的山谷里去吧，在那里，一生的收获将会成熟为黄金的智慧。

321

Things look phantastic in this dimness of the dusk——the spires whose bases are lost in the dark and tree tops like blots of ink.

I shall wait for the morning and wake up to see thy city in the light.

在这黄昏的朦胧里，好些东西看起来都仿佛是幻象一般——尖塔的底层在黑暗里消失了，树顶像是墨水的斑点似的。

我将等待着黎明，当我醒来的时候，就会看到在光明里的您的城市。

322

I have suffered and despaired and known death and I am glad that I am in this great world.

我曾经受苦过，曾经失望过，曾经体会过“死亡”，于是我以我在这伟大的世界里为乐。

323

There are tracts in my life that are bare and silent. They are the open spaces where my busy days had their light and air.

在我的一生里，也有贫乏和沉默的地域。它们是我在忙碌的日子里得到日光与空气的几片空旷之地。

324

Release me from my unfulfilled past clinging to me from behind making death difficult.

我未完成的过去，从后边缠绕到我身上，使我难于死去，请从它那里释放了我吧。

325

Let this be my last word，that I trust thy love.

“我相信你的爱。”让这句话做我最后的话。

图文资讯
拓展书籍内容，开阔阅读视野。
拓展视频
观看在线视频，激发阅读兴趣。
阅读分享
分享阅读心得，碰撞思维火花。
趣味测评
测评阅读习惯，获取阅读建议。